igloobooks

Published in 2014
by Igloo Books Ltd
Cottage Farm
Sywell
NN6 0BJ
www.igloobooks.com

GUA006 0914
4 6 8 10 9 7 5 3
ISBN: 978-1-78197-104-8

Illustrated by Emma Foster

Printed and manufactured in China

My Sweetest
Princess
Story

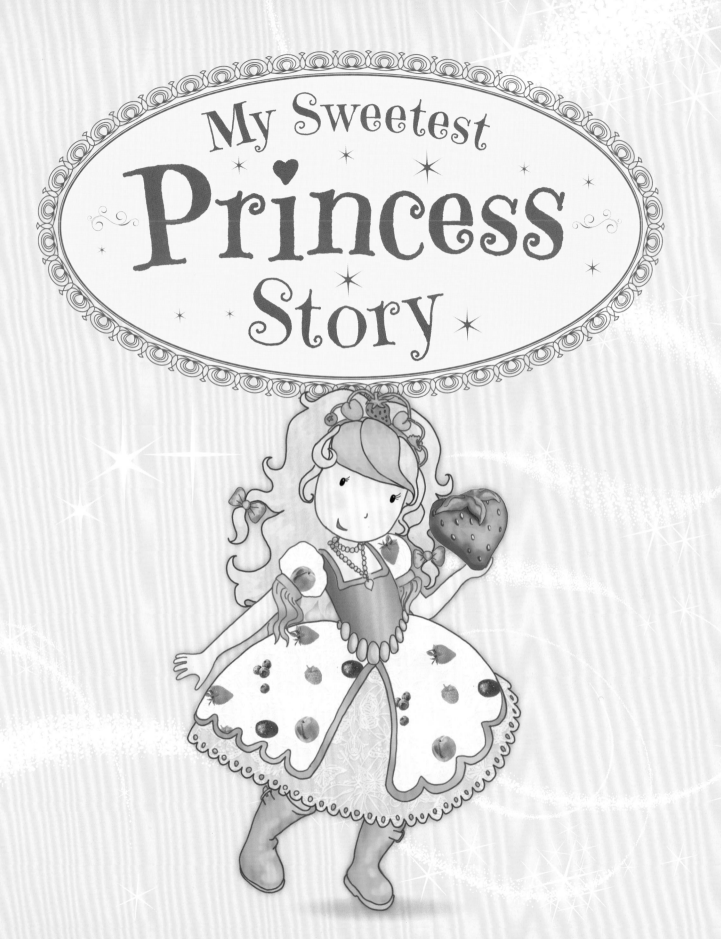

igloobooks

Princess Polly loved to eat strawberries more than anything else
in the world. For breakfast, she would gobble down stacks of strawberry
pancakes, with oozy strawberry sauce. Then, she would munch a
couple of sticky, pink strawberry cupcakes.

The king and queen were worried about Polly. "Don't you want to try eating other things, without strawberries?" they asked the princess, as she slurped down a thick, gloopy strawberry milkshake. "No, thank you," said Princess Polly. "Strawberries are the best."

After breakfast, Princess Polly usually wanted to eat even more strawberry treats. She would sneak to the kitchen, where the royal chef would happily make her a strawberry sundae, or strawberry sandwiches. He sometimes even made strawberry pizza, with extra-sugary sauce.

Princess Polly munched her way through so many strawberries that she even had her own strawberry fields, stretching right across the palace grounds. "I'm so happy to have so many strawberries all to myself," thought Princess Polly, gazing out of her bedroom window.

Then, one day, something terrible happened. Princess Polly was out walking with the king and queen, when she spotted a gigantic flock of birds circling above her strawberry fields. "I wonder what they're doing," Polly thought to herself, looking up at the sky curiously.

Suddenly, hundreds of birds swooped down and started to snatch up
Princess Polly's strawberries with their beaks. "Stop it!" shrieked Polly.
"Leave my strawberries alone!" The greedy birds didn't listen. In no time
at all, they had gobbled down every last one of Polly's strawberries.

Without strawberries, Princess Polly refused to eat anything at all. The king and queen tried to think of ways to tempt Polly into eating something new. "Don't worry," said the royal chef. "I'll cook some fantastic new dishes." Soon, he had filled the dining table with strange and exciting meals.

"Try this pizza covered with sweets, Polly," suggested the queen.
"Or some chicken, with a squashy pink marshmallow," said the king.
The chef brought the princess crunchy carrot cupcakes and a cherry and
chocolate swiss roll. He even made jelly with chips and a raspberry and
sausage tart, but Polly just crossed her arms and frowned.

Later, after lots of banging about in the kitchen, the royal chef wheeled out an enormous cake. It was covered in purple jelly and stuffed full of peanuts. "I made my very special peanut butter and jelly cake just for you, Princess," said the royal chef, puffing out his chest proudly.

Princess Polly thought the cake looked horrible. It didn't have any strawberries in it at all. She gave it a little poke and with a big SQUISH, a blob of purple jelly came squelching from the cake and splatted right onto Princess Polly's face.

Princess Polly took the cake from the royal chef, but only so that everyone would leave her alone. "I'm not eating that mountain of peanut gloop, Smudge," she told her puppy. "It hasn't got any strawberries in it at all." To Smudge's delight, Princess Polly gave him slice after slice of peanut cake, until the whole thing had gone.

That evening, the king and queen were holding a grand feast and everyone was busy preparing for the guests to arrive. The royal seamstress had even made Princess Polly a special dress to wear. When the queen brought it up to her bedroom, Polly just cried, "There won't be any strawberries at the feast, so I'm not going!"

As Princess Polly sat and sulked in her bedroom, she could smell all the food from the grand feast. "It's making my tummy growl and gurgle," moaned Polly. Soon, she was so hungry that she couldn't bear it, so Polly decided to creep downstairs and see if there was anything for her to eat.

When she reached the bottom of the grand staircase, Princess
Polly peeked into the dining room. She listened to all of the king and
queen's guests laughing and saying how delicious the food tasted.
As she hid behind the wall, the yummy smells became so strong
that Polly's mouth started to water.

Polly wanted to get a better look at the dishes that the guests were eating. "Why does everything smell so tasty, when there isn't a single strawberry in sight?" she wondered. Quietly, the princess crept into the dining room. Before anybody noticed, she crawled underneath the table to hide.

Princess Polly peeked over the dining table and couldn't believe
how many unusual things she could see. Everything looked amazing!
Sneakily, Polly snatched a bowl of blueberries, some chocolate cupcakes,
a few sandwiches and a hot dog, then scrambled back under the table.

First, Princess Polly decided to try a gooey chocolate cupcake. She took a small bite and couldn't believe how scrummy the chocolate icing was! After gobbling down the rest of the cupcake, Polly nibbled her way through a crunchy cucumber sandwich, which was very tasty, too.

Next, Polly ate an extra-saucy hot dog, dripping with mustard and tomato sauce. Smudge was enjoying the food from the feast, too. He had just munched his way through a juicy peach, when Princess Polly grabbed a handful of plump blueberries from the bowl. Wondering what exactly they were, she popped a berry into her mouth. "Wow!" cried Polly. "This is even yummier than a strawberry!"

Princess Polly suddenly realised that she had spoken very loudly. Everyone must have heard her! "Who's under the table?" said one of the guests, sounding puzzled. The king lifted up the long tablecloth and saw Polly underneath, with blueberry juice all around her mouth.

"What on earth are you hiding under the table for, Polly?" asked
the queen. Feeling embarrased, Princess Polly told the queen how hungry
she had been and how much she liked the blueberries. "They're delicious,"
she said. "I'm sorry for not trying to eat the food you brought me earlier."

The next day, Princess Polly couldn't wait until dinner time. The royal chef whipped up every lovely dish that Polly had refused before, plus lots of extra-special treats. There was a blueberry tart, a blueberry pie and even a blueberry sundae. "Oh, thank you!" said Polly to the royal chef.

"I'm glad that the birds ate my strawberries," Princess Polly told the king and queen, through a mouthful of chocolate cupcake. "Otherwise, I would never have tried blueberries or peaches, or any of the other yummy things I've eaten since yesterday."

With help from the royal gardeners, Princess Polly planted all sorts of different fruit across the palace grounds. She grew juicy grapes, sweet raspberries and even the biggest watermelons in the whole kingdom.

Best of all, Princess Polly loved to share her fruit with everyone. The king and queen were very proud of Polly for trying lots of different food, but they were even prouder of what a generous princess she had become after all.

Scratch here ⟶